HER CHRISTMAS CAROLE

MARGAUX FOX

1

1995

There was this summer in 1995 when their whole lives lay ahead of them. On Jo's 17th birthday, Carole and Jo ran through the corn field playing chase with each other. Jo's two border collies ran with them, the sun on their backs, the breeze in their faces. They fell into the long grassy bank at the edge of the field laughing and Carole's smile and green eyes were lit up in the sunlight, she had never looked more beautiful. Jo leaned over and kissed her. Carole felt it everywhere and kissed her back, lost in the warm summer haze. Lost in Jo's summer haze. The sun a golden halo above Jo's sandy hair. Jo came up for air and smiled widely. Then back to kissing Carole. Bodies intertwined, hands roaming. Teenage lust abounded.

THEY THOUGHT they would be together forever. They thought life could always be like that. They were wrong. So very wrong.

2

2019

Joanna Dale glanced at her phone again. It was an old iPhone with a screen so cracked and dirty she could barely decipher the message.

TEXT FROM THE BANK:

You are overdrawn. Please pay funds into your account before 2.30pm to avoid further charges.

JO IGNORED IT. She was very good at ignoring both letters and texts demanding money. She had a mountain of mail that she was ignoring. Envelopes unopened. Angry red lettering demanding attention that it just wasn't going to get. She threw on her wellies and her dirty fleece and stormed out of the old farmhouse. There was a fence that needed fixing, the sheep had escaped again and it couldn't wait. Roux, the border collie followed her and jumped in the old Land Rover next to her. She pushed her red and white face through the open window and joyously panted in the breeze as they bumped along the track towards the sheep field.

Jo squelched through the autumn mud with her power tools and set to work on the broken fence. Another patch up job, but it was the best she could do. New fences were expensive. Jo was very good at fixing things. For years she had learnt from her father. Westdale Farm had always struggled, so machinery, fences and buildings were repaired rather than replaced. The farmhouse was in trouble too- in dire need of a new roof. Jo had been out on the roof again this morning to replace a lost tile and try to stop the leaking, but it was becoming futile. And perhaps she was getting a little old for scrambling around rooftops. Damp patches covered all of the ceilings and the house just did not cope with the constant rain that there had been lately. Her father had taught her well on many things, a very practical man, good with the animals, unfortunately a useless businessman. Jo had grown up very like him. She was tall and strong and her rough hands were very skilled, but saving a failing business was not her forte.

Her phone rang and she squinted at the cracked screen:

DAD

SHE SWIPED to accept the call and put him on speaker as she worked on the fence. The weather was definitely cooling off-winter was coming.

"Joanna," he said, then a pause, then "How are the new cattle? Are they still in the riverside field? Fine beasts they are."

"They are putting on weight well Dad. Fine beasts, you are right. You chose them well," she replied.

"Wonderful," he said. "Just wonderful."

She imagined him happy and proud of the cattle he had chosen. He had always been such a proud man. He had always had an eye for quality animals. It broke her heart to think too hard about where he was now. There were no cattle on the farm anymore. There hadn't been for thirty years. But she didn't have the heart to tell him. There was no riverside field anymore either. Jo had had to sell it recently along with a lot of other land to pay off debts when she took over the running of the farm. Arthur Dale had been diagnosed with dementia and eventually she couldn't care for him anymore and he was moved into a home.

"How's your mother?" he asked hopefully.

Still dead, Jo thought sadly. But she replied kindly, "She's just making dinner Dad, she can't make it to the phone."

"OK darling. I know you'll have a busy day. That farm won't run itself." He was right about one thing at least. The jobs never ended. "Bye Jo."

"Bye Dad." Emotion was hard to feel for Jo. It was trapped deep under the surface and she never let it out. There really wasn't time for emotion.

. . .

SHE SHOVED her phone in her pocket and put her whistle to her lips and sent Roux across the land to fetch the sheep. The whistle a gift from Carole so many years ago. She felt their engraved names on it with her tongue. Roux went straight to work, her red and white fur a streak against the green of the grass. Jo whistled loudly and Roux worked to tighten the sheep into a group and move them back towards the gate of their field. Roux ran backwards and forwards, always alert for her next command. She was an incredible dog, the best Jo had seen. She was a pup from Arthur's old working dogs, but she was better than either of her parents had been. She was fast, lean and athletic. She was so eager to please and clever, quick, kind but firm with the sheep. She had a calming effect on the sheep. The perfect working dog. Jo had won the national sheepdog trials last year with her as a I year old and been offered a lot of money to sell her.

A truly great sheepdog is hard to find and is a very valuable asset to a farm. A champion working dog like Roux was wasted really on Westdale Farm. They didn't have that many sheep anymore comparative to other farms. Part sheep farm, part arable now. Over the years Jo had been forced to sell more land in order to keep the farm afloat. Jo adored Roux. She couldn't bear to sell her. Roux was really her only constant now. Arthur had been ill for years and Jo had done her best to care for him. Now he was gone too, the big house was so lonely. Roux was Jo's shadow. The thought of losing her too was too much.

Roux brought the sheep back through the five bar gate as Jo held it open. Sometimes she genuinely thought Roux understood full sentences. She pushed the gate to and lifted it into place, another job done for the day.

It had become a lonely existence farming alone. Even for an introvert like Jo, it could be desolate in the cold winters. The summers were better, she would hire help in over harvest and the sun itself made outdoor working a pleasure. But at 41 years old and barely scraping by financially, Jo began to wonder what the next 20 years would look like. Just her, working away by herself, just about making enough money to keep herself and her beloved dog.

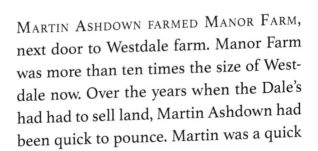

MARTIN ASHDOWN FARMED MANOR FARM, next door to Westdale farm. Manor Farm was more than ten times the size of Westdale now. Over the years when the Dale's had had to sell land, Martin Ashdown had been quick to pounce. Martin was a quick and astute business man with a thriving sheep farm and a successful arable side. Martin was quick to know what would sell well and always seemed to be one step ahead with what he was growing. Martin had many farm workers now, his own hands were never dirty.

His daughter Carole had grown up on the farm but gone to an expensive boarding school. She was a year older than Jo. Carole went to Cambridge University studying business and then moved to London and eventually became Head of Marketing for a big IT company. Carole was intelligent, quick to learn and pushed from a young age by her father to be a success.

3

2019

Carole was still in London. She rented a stunning apartment that overlooked the Thames. She sat on her balcony in the early evening darkness with a large glass of gin while mindlessly working her way through the dating app on her phone.

LEFT SWIPE.
Left Swipe.
Left Swipe.

. . .

SHE SIPPED her gin as she contemplated her life, ice clunking against glass.

Dating was the one area of Carole's life that continued to be a failure. And Carole wasn't a failing kind of woman. Carole was successful in everything she put her mind to, but she just couldn't manage to make a relationship a success.

She had had girlfriends over the years. But she never really felt happy. Never really felt settled with any of them. She had tried women similar to her- career focussed, high earning. They would argue constantly, their relationships turbulent and full of resentment. Both partners too competitive to ever back down. She had tried younger women, less driven women, but she ended up hating their frivolous whimsical natures or their lack of passion.

She had a date that night so she slipped into a tight black sheath dress that reached just below the knee and clung to every curve in sight. She slipped on her plain black heels and some mascara and a bold red lipstick. Her hair like rich dark chocolate, shoulder length, was in casual waves that had taken her an hour to create. She looked amazing and she knew it. Carole's age was hard to pin. From a distance she could have been ten years younger. Only when you looked closely could you see the fine lines around her eyes and the toll the years had taken.

Her phone notified her that her Uber had arrived and she grabbed her wool coat and headed out into the night.

She had arranged to meet her date in her favourite cocktail bar. It was a classy, modern bar.

Kelly, 32, owns her own plumbing business.

KELLY ONLINE LOOKED dapper in a suit.

Butch, strong and masculine. Carole always enjoyed a certain masculinity in a woman. Part of her wished she had lived in the time when the butch-femme dynamic was prevalent. These days there was so much variety in lesbians and a real old school butch was hard to find. Carole embraced life as a high femme. Carole was always immaculate and feminine and always with grace.

Carole drank gin. Her drinking habits were always predictable. Never lured by the fancy cocktails, Carole enjoyed a classic G and T. Always with fresh lime. Plenty of ice and lime. The barmaids knew her and she had tipped them enough that she never had to ask any more. Her drink was made and brought over to her as soon as she walked in and sat down. Carole always enjoyed the pretty barmaids. The owner of this bar had got it right. Young, attractive, friendly barmaids. Interestingly, no male staff. Just pretty young girls.

Carole looked around the tables at the clientele. Mostly business men. Some with younger women. Probably not their wives.

Carole turned around and there was Kelly. Tight Levis, a Ralph Lauren masculine white shirt and cufflinks sparkling at her wrists- a nice touch. The clothes fitted tight to her muscular body, Kelly was just what Carole wanted tonight. The barmaid was at their table immediately, addressed Kelly as 'Sir' and asked politely what she could get for her. Kelly wasn't phased by the 'Sir' and Carole smiled to herself- she found that attractive.

Kelly ordered a pint of Guinness. None of the trendy 'craft' beer that Carole abhorred. Carole thought they might get along just fine.

And they did.

They talked and laughed through the evening. They went for dinner together.

"What do you love the most?" Carole asked.

"Steak," replied Kelly.

Of course Carole knew the best steak restaurant and they knew her and they were swept quickly to a great table overlooking the rest of the restaurant.

Kelly was charming and gentlemanly throughout. They finished dinner and Carole raised her green eyes under the long black lashes and looked directly at Kelly. Her eyes burned into Kelly's with an intensity she had never known.

"I've ordered an Uber. Come home with me."

Kelly had never met anyone quite like Carole. Carole's body in that tight dress.

Her rouged full lips. Her confidence. Kelly had never met a woman so alpha. As a butch there was this common assumption that she would be dominant, that she would be alpha, and here was this dazzling femme taking all that pressure from her shoulders. The whole combination was intoxicating to Kelly and she went home with Carole.

As the taxi pulled up at Carole's apartment, Kelly was momentarily intimidated by the splendour but hid it well. Not before Carole noticed, but she was used to noticing things like that in people she brought home. She could see Kelly doing the maths in her head of how much the apartment was worth. She was probably still well off in her valuation. Places like this overlooking the river cost more than the average person could imagine.

Carole earned a huge salary and she loved to spend it.

In the minimalist white kitchen, Kelly

gazed out of the big glass doors at the lights on the river.

Carole made them both a gin, never asking if Kelly liked it.

ICE CLINKED LOUDLY in the silence. Carole's big kitchen knife on the chopping board, limes quartered and added to the drinks.

Carole led Kelly to her bedroom, sexual tension high. Inhibitions low.

The bedsheets were black and smooth and expensive looking like rich black coffee.

Carole went to a wooden chest at the end of her bed and pulled out a strap on harness and dildo and threw them to Kelly.

"Put these on," she ordered.

Kelly felt the black leather of the harness supple in her hands, the dildo silicone yet weighty. She had never known anything quite like this, but it excited her beyond anything else. She stripped and obeyed instructions as she watched Carole peel off her dress and hang it up.

Carole's underwear was red lace. It matched her lipstick and that was no accident.

"Fuck me," she said, in full control of the situation. "I don't want to have to ask twice."

Kelly didn't need telling twice. Carole was a woman who knew exactly what she wanted and was clearly used to getting it. Kelly pulled Carole to her and turned her round.

SHE PULLED her underwear down over her round ass and bent her forwards pushing her face to the bed as she entered her with the big strap on.

Carole was ready and wanting. The

dinner and the gin were the foreplay to Carole. She was wet and anticipating.

Kelly fucked her in many positions. Carole demanded harder and got it. Carole demanded more and got it.

Carole's full breasts spilled from her bra and moved as they fucked. Kelly felt grateful she was fit and strong as she began to understand how demanding Carole could be.

Carole asked for Kelly's tongue. Kelly's mouth hot and wet against her. She pulled Kelly's face tight in against her. She orgasmed hard for Kelly's mouth and just as she did Kelly came against the leather straps tight between her legs.

Kelly gasped and smiled and came up for air. This woman was something else entirely.

Carole pulled Kelly up to her and for a minute they lay entwined, Kelly's head against Carole's breast. She breathed in the scent of her and the scent of her sex.

Carole picked up her phone and Kelly vaguely heard her tapping the screen.

"I've ordered you an Uber. I have an early morning. I hope you don't mind. I had a really great time, thank you." said Carole.

AND JUST LIKE THAT, Kelly was dismissed.

THERE HAD BEEN many Kellys lately. Almost interchangeable. Masculine. Fit looking. Younger than her. Butch, but clearly not a natural top. Carole enjoyed sex and liked particular things sexually. These women seemed more than happy to be used by her for an evening or two of fine food and drink and hot sex. Carole never kissed them.

. . .

IT HAD BEEN years since Carole had had a real relationship. On some level she knew that she was using these women to fill a void in her life. She was using rough sex to help her to feel something.

THERE WERE STILL plenty of evenings spent alone, when dating apps couldn't come up with a good looking woman for her to spend the evening with. She was reluctant to use the same woman too much for fear of giving them the wrong impression- that there was potential of anything more. There really wasn't. She had nothing more to give than her body.

4

1994

When they were teenagers Jo and Carole became friends. Growing up on neighbouring farms, they knew of each other but their paths had rarely crossed. Their fathers were reluctant friends. Martin Ashdown was very charming, the astute businessman, keen to keep Jo's father Arthur onside because he knew Arthur was struggling financially and he wanted to buy land from Arthur's farm. Arthur was not overly fond of Martin, but he was not aware of Martin's underlying motives for the friendship.

Jo was sixteen years old and keen to finish school and get to working full time on the farm. She woke early that morning a week before Christmas to check on Belle, one of the working sheepdogs. Belle was pregnant and Jo had been sure when she went to bed last night that the birth was imminent. Belle had been restless and refused her dinner. Jo pulled on her warm winter pyjamas and some thick socks and ran downstairs in the cold farmhouse. She could see her own breath in the cold air. She opened the door to the utility room to see Belle panting and straining. She had been right! The pups were coming. Jo got towels and a bowl of warm water ready and sat on the floor soothing the distressed dog. It was Belle's first litter and she seemed confused by what was happening to her body. Soon enough, the first pup appeared, tiny alien face first covered in membrane. She slid out and Jo broke the membrane around her face.

"I'm happy to see you little pup," smiled Jo as the pup started moving and seeking out milk.

Arthur popped his head round the door along with Red who was the father of the pups and he smiled to see Jo handling Belle and the birth so well.

"I'm heading out to the sheep. I'll be back soon," he said.

Seven pups later and Belle began to settle and her breathing calmed. She started to clean her pups and Jo gently helped the pups to locate nipples to start feeding.

Jo set them up a little pen and bed next to the AGA in the kitchen and she cleaned up. The big range cooker was the best source of heat. Belle seemed grateful and exhausted as she settled into her new bed adjusting to her new role as a mother.

Jo felt as proud as if she had given birth to the pups herself. Eight perfect healthy little furballs snuggled into their mother. Five black and white. Three red and white.

Jo was to get one of the pups to keep for herself and train up as a working sheepdog. She couldn't wait to have a puppy of her very own to train. She looked at the eight pups carefully, imagining them as adults, thinking of what their names might be. Thinking of what their personalities might be.

It was 8.30am.

Jo ran upstairs shouting, "Mum, the puppies are here!"

"MUM."

There was no answer. Strange, thought Jo.

"MUM."

Jo ran into her parents bedroom to see her mum still in bed. Her mum was always an early riser who liked to get up as dawn came through her bedroom windows.

"Mum, the puppies have been born. Belle did so well, she will make a great mum! There are eight of them! Come and see!"

There was no answer.

Jo's mother was asleep on her side and Jo pulled at her shoulder pulling her onto her back.

Her body rolled lifelessly.

Her eyes stared glassy and vacant.

Her body was as cold as ice.

Jo's mother was dead.

5

1994

Christmas 1994

The year that Jo's mother died was the first year that Carole's family invited Jo and Arthur to their home for Christmas day. The doctors said sometimes it happens, that people just die in their sleep. That they have a heart condition or something else and they just die.

How could she just die?

Jo couldn't understand any of it. But as it was nearly Christmas, the autopsy would have to wait until January. There had been police, the local village police and then some more important police. There had been questions, so many questions. A very brief investigation which found nothing suspicious. Then Jo and her father were left alone for the two dead weeks of Christmas and New Year and told they would be contacted in January.

Some people just die apparently.

She was fine. She was fit and well. She was fine the evening previous. She was planning Christmas day, it was always just the three of them and the dogs. There was laughter and lots of food and silly games. She was fine.

And then she was dead.

Jo and Arthur were desolate.

Lost in their own personal despairs. No idea how to support or even talk to each other. They slipped back into life, keeping the farm alive, caring for the animals. Jo caring for the new puppies. Crying quietly into their soft fur all alone.

Jo's mother was full of life, full of fun,

a traditional farmer's wife always found making food. Soups, breads, stews, Sunday roasts. She had been such a loving, caring mother and wife. Jo's mother was the beating heart of the farmhouse.

It was so quiet without her.

Christmas day came and there was a light snowfall across the countryside. A Christmas card perfect scene. Jo and Arthur walked across the fields to the Manor Farm House where fairy lights twinkled and warm laughter spilled out. A true family Christmas.

Anne Ashdown threw open the door and welcomed them in. She threw her arms around Jo and enveloped her in a huge hug.

"Joanna, my darling, I'm so pleased you could make it." Jo's awkward scrawny body rigid in the hug. A sticky lipstick kiss pushed onto her cheek. Jo felt numb.

Arthur received a similar welcome and was similarly awkward.

They were welcomed into a big hallway and glasses of champagne thrust into their hands and they hadn't quite anticipated the amount of people who would be there.

"Martin and Carole, you know. This is my sister Marsha, and her husband and children. Martin's mother and father. My mother. Martin's brother and his wife and children." Anne went on and on and Jo and Arthur both stared vacantly.

Then Carole came up to Jo and took her hand.

"JoJo. Come with me. There's too many people in here. You must be exhausted." Carole was glamorous suddenly. A different Carole than the one she had met before. A grown up Carole. It was as if overnight, Carole had become a woman. A tight red sweater that clung to full breasts and a black pencil skirt. And heels. And make up. But still her beautiful dark hair a long wavy cloud.

Still her kind green eyes that wanted to care for Jo.

Carole lead her out of the back door of their big house.

"Do you want to go for a walk before lunch JoJo?" she said. They were in garage where the boots were stored, Carole pulled out two pairs of wellington boots and pulled a couple of coats off the coat rack. Just like any farmhouse, there was always a huge assortment of coats and boots and nobody was ever quite sure where they all came from.

Jo pulled on the boots and coat. Still awkward in jeans and an old Christmas jumper that her mum had knitted. The sleeves were a little too short on it now.

Carole kicked off her heels and pulled wellies over her tights. The two of them walked out into the snow.

Carole's family had a black labrador and a border collie that lived in a large kennel outside. They weren't allowed in the house. Carole's mother was very house proud. The house was always immaculate and there was no time for dog hair or muddy paw prints. Both came along for the journey, happy to be out and running around.

They walked along the snowy track towards the river. And talked.

Carole was the first person to talk to Jo. To really talk to her like a human being. To ask her about that morning. About her mother. To ask her how she felt. How she was coping. Jo and her father had barely spoken since it happened. Neither of them had the words.

There was a felled thick tree trunk next to the river that the two girls sat on. Snow crunching under their bums as they sat down. The dogs played nearby.

"My hands are freezing," Jo said, rubbing them against each other.

"Give them here," said Carole taking Jo's hands in her own.

Jo watched Carole's long delicate fingers and painted dark red nails holding her own rough hands and she was momentarily ashamed of her hardworking hands. Carole's hands were somehow warm and welcoming. She held Jo's pale fingers tight. Then she rubbed them carefully, firmly but gently and as they began to warm up she ran her fingers across the ridges and dry skin.

Carole noticed the strength in Jo's hands compared to her own. There were scratches and sores from the work that she did. Carole wanted to soothe and care for her hardworking hands.

Carole lifted Jo's hands to her mouth and blew on them. Their eyes met for a moment and Carole kissed her hands lightly.

A moment that meant so much. A moment that twenty five years later, they could both remember so vividly.

Jo looked away first. Carole was so

beautiful. Carole had been so kind to her. The feelings she felt for her in that moment were too much to process. Too much to imagine.

They both got up and headed back to the house for Christmas lunch.

CAROLE WENT BACK to boarding school after Christmas and Jo back to school and the farm. Life went back to normal for both of them. Normal except for Westdale farm was a different place without Jo's mother. Normal except for Jo's feelings for Carole were growing and growing and she had no idea what to do about it.

6

1995

It was May and there had been no real clarity on how Jo's mother died. The autopsy said it was her heart.

Some people just die.

Jo focussed all her attention on her black and white border collie pup Jake. She had a big manual on how to train sheepdogs and she had learnt a lot from her father. She would spend time in the fields with Jake and her manual, short bursts of learning for Jake. Then home to the empty house. They had three dogs now, Belle, Red and Jake. Belle's other puppies had been sold and had made them enough money to buy the parts they needed to fix the tractor.

Carole wrote to Jo in May. A morning like any other, the early summer sun beginning to shine, Jo walked to the end of the farm drive to collect the mail and was excited to see a handwritten envelope for her. She sat under a cherry tree with the dogs, surrounded by pink blossom and read the letter. Her handwriting was loopy and extravagant- very Carole.

Dear JoJo,

Carole had taken to calling her JoJo and Jo wasn't quite sure why. But she liked it. She was always just Jo. Joanna had never suited her. She always imagined a Joanna to have blonde plaits and pink dresses. JoJo made her different. Special.

Carole spoke of her boarding school and it seemed like another world that Jo couldn't quite understand. Carole was acing all her subjects, which was no surprise. She told Jo she thought about her often and wondered how she was doing. She asked about Belle's puppies. She asked about Jo's father. At the end of the letter, she said....

I miss you JoJo. I would love to spend time over the summer with you and get to know you more.
With Love,
Carole

Jo's heart leapt. Maybe Carole liked her in the way that she liked Carole. She would write back. She smiled and jumped up excited for her work for the day. Wishing for the days to pass so it could be summer and Carole could be home.

1995

It was a bright June day and Carole was packed and on her way home from boarding school in the back of the smart new Range Rover with Martin driving and Anne chatting away to her and asking her how things had been. Carole was friendly and polite and answered her parents questions. She couldn't wait to get home and go and see Jo. Jo had been all she could think about while she was away. There was something about how awkward and geeky she was. Her passion for training her dogs and working the farm. And those big sad brown eyes. Carole was starting to get a lot of attention from men. An all girls school limited her encounters with men, but the way the curves of her body had developed and the tight clothes she liked to wear drew a lot of attention. But ironically, she wasn't interested in men. She loved the way Jo looked at her. Both in an obvious way, at her breasts or her lips and in the way that Jo saw more of her and wanted more of her. She liked Jo's nervousness around her and the way she blushed and jumped ever so slightly when Carole touched her. As though Carole's touch was electric and Jo felt it everywhere.

Carole didn't know much about lesbians so she researched. She knew for sure that her desires were female only. She even found some old books featuring lesbian relationships in the school library. She laughed as she was sure the school would have no idea that they had books like this in their library. And she devoured them. She practiced kissing on her friend Susie at school in the dormitory and she liked it.

Kissing Jo was something she thought about late at night in her bed at school. The thought of Jo's lean body naked against her own. Carole touched herself to orgasm many nights. Sharing a room, she tried so hard to stay quiet but she heard her own whimper as she came.

The Range Rover finally pulled in to

the driveway home at Manor Farm. Carole could see Westdale Farm across the fields and wondered if she could get away this evening to see Jo.

"Mum, I'd like to pop over and see Joanna Dale this evening if that is ok? I've been terribly worried about her since Mrs Dale died, I'd like to try and be a good friend."

"Thats a lovely idea Carole. We will have an early supper and you can go after that."

Carole smiled to herself and looked at her watch. Early supper could be 5.30. She could head over at 6pm.

It was ten minutes past six when Carole managed to escape. She pulled on chino shorts and a white T shirt that cut low and exposed a good amount of her full breasts. She brushed her long dark mane till it shone. She put some light make up on, mascara accentuating her eyes and an alluring shiny gloss on her lips. It took a bit of effort to make herself look effortlessly beautiful. She wanted to wear her wedge heeled sandals but she also wanted to run across the fields, so practicality and her trainers won. Her long brown legs looked good in the shorts.

She ran across the fields to Westdale Farm and the bright summer evening was still warm as she knocked on the door. The dogs barked and it was a couple of minutes before Jo came to the door in dirty denim shorts looking taller than she did before, her arms and legs nut brown, her hair lighter from the sun tied up in a messy ponytail.

Her face lit up and beamed a huge smile as she saw it was Carole. Her sad eyes became hope.

Carole hugged her.

It might have been a small moment, but for Jo, it was the first time they had hugged. Feeling Carole's warm body that close and her breasts pressing into Jo was everything she had dreamed of. Carole's perfume was citrus mingling with the scent of her. She was shorter than Jo, but only by a little.

Jo breathed her in.

Jo's father was still out in the fields.

"It's so great to see you JoJo," Carole said as she released the hug.

"Would you like a drink?" Jo asked awkwardly.

"Have you got alcohol?" Carole asked.

"I mean, there's a cabinet with alcohol in. I'm not sure what there is." Jo had never really drunk before, but she lead Carole to her parents alcohol cupboard.

Carole immediately took the lead and found a pretty full green glass bottle of 'London Dry Gin'. Jo couldn't remember seeing anyone drink gin. Her mother would sometimes have wine. Her father would have beer or whisky on the odd occasion. Carole found an open bottle of flat lemonade and some lime cordial.

Jo admired her resourcefulness. They took their drinks outside and sat on the stone wall separating the garden from the fields.

Soon they were giggly from the gin and the awkwardness was gone. It was as if they had known each other forever.

Carole told Jo stories from boarding school. Jo told stories from the farm and stories of the dogs.

Carole touched Jo's hand and the warmth radiated through her.

Carole looked at Jo, her face backed by the lazy evening sunshine. Jo's hair was escaping the elastic, her jawline was strong and square and her dark eyes big and expectant.

Carole kissed her.

8

2019

It was a crisp cold morning, the 1st of December, the temperature had really started to drop. Frost was on the grass. Jo walked down to the end of the drive to collect the mail as she did every morning, Roux trotted along ahead.

Jo opened the mailbox and there it was. A red envelope with Carole's familiar loopy handwriting.

JoJo Dale
Westdale Farm

EVERY YEAR in early December a Christmas card would arrive from Carole. 1995 was the first, then every year since.

25 YEARS, 25 Christmas cards.

Always in a red envelope. Always addressed to 'JoJo'. There was always a handwritten letter inside detailing Carole's year. Always questions about Jo's life, the farm, her father, the dogs. More personal than an acquaintance, but over the years, Christmas gradually became the only time that Carole contacted her. The Christmas letter and then Christmas day itself at Carole's family home.

The letter would always be signed off the same way.

With Love,
At Christmas,
Carole

9

2019

Jo would respond faithfully, with a letter detailing her own year. Her own life captured in a couple pieces of paper. A year at a time. Jo sent very few christmas cards and only wrote letters to Carole. One a year in response to Carole's letter. Carole had made it crystal clear all those years ago that there was to be nothing between them again, yet still these annual letters bound them. Still this *'With Love, At Christmas.'* from Carole. Every year the same words. Every year brought back memories. Every year, Jo read the letter carefully and replied immediately.

Every year since her mother's death, Anne Ashdown faithfully invited Jo and her father to the big family gathering at their home on Christmas day. Carole would always come home for Christmas. She hadn't missed a single one.

Over the years, Carole had had girlfriends. In the past ten years she had even brought a couple of girlfriends home at Christmas. Anne would look uncomfortable and Martin would be in complete denial. They would pretend that she was Carole's 'friend'. The rest of their family wasn't stupid. Carole had never married, never brought home a man. Then sometimes she would turn up with a masculine looking woman. A woman who 'looked like a lesbian'. Although neither Carole or Jo had ever bought into that. Sexual orientation was about who you desired, not how you cut your hair and the clothes you wore.

This year's letter was a bit different.

Dear JoJo,

I have had another busy year with work. I've been promoted, I'm now at head of Marketing and New Business which is a great place to be really. It is everything I have worked towards and I feel like I really have the responsibility and the power that I deserve now. I spent a couple of months in Sydney early in the year, helping to set up the Australian office to run an Australian branch of the company. Work put me up in an incredible apartment backing onto Manly Beach. Amazing views of the beach and the ocean- you would have loved it.

I sometimes imagine the 'us' of years ago. Running around through the countryside and the fun we used to have! I ran around on the beach in Australia. I ran into the ocean feeling like I was eighteen again. There was something about the freedom, swimming in the sea, letting the waves wash over me, just being alone there- there was something magical about it. I don't do so much stuff like that these days, but then maybe this is a sign I should do more.

Anyway, then I was back to London life. Which has been much the same as usual. There's work- we have expanded to a bigger building. I got a bigger office with the new position too, I'm on the 18th floor. I have great views of the city! You would hate London. Have you ever been? You could visit me sometime?

I've been dating a bit, but nothing serious. I'm beginning to think I am just destined to be alone forever!

My parents are much the same. I mean, you probably see them more than I do. To be honest, I've not seen them since last Christmas.

How is everything with the farm? And lovely Roux- please do bring her along for

Christmas day. Have you dated anyone this year? I'd love to hear everything.

I'm actually planning to be home for my dad's birthday next weekend. They are having a party for his 70th and they've invited me and asked me to bring a 'friend'. So I thought of you obviously. It is on the 7th at theirs. I would love you to come if you are free.

I'm looking forward to seeing you.

I miss you.

With Love,
At Christmas,
Carole

10

2019

This year's letter was different. The recollection of *the 'us' of years ago*

THE '*I MISS YOU*'

The invitation to visit London- Carole had lived in London for twenty years and never invited Jo.

The invitation to her father's party- Jo had literally only seen Carole on Christmas day for so many years.

And yet, this letter. This year. Things

seemed different. Jo wasn't sure how to feel about it.

But she text Carole and said she would see her at her father's party.

WHAT DID CAROLE WANT?

11

1995

It was a warm summer evening and Carole and Jo walked together excitedly to the big barn that was next to the river field where the sheep were. It was used to store hay and they could smell the freshly cut bales as they walked in. Plenty of hay to keep the pregnant ewes well fed through the winter. Arthur was harvesting with his men on the other side of the farm, the good weather meaning they worked late into the evening. They had left the dogs at the house. Jo had carefully chosen somewhere far out of sight and out of mind. Somewhere she knew they could be alone. Completely alone.

Behind a wall of hay bales, Jo opened her rucksack. She knelt down and carefully spread out two tartan picnic blankets over the soft bed of hay on the floor. Carole smiled as she watched, her dark hair glossy in the sun. Jo looked nervous and a little unsure. They had talked about it so much. What they would do when they could be completely alone. They had thought about it. Each of them. In the quiet of their own bed late at night. But here and now, Jo was nervous. The evening light, still bright, shone in through the slats of the barn walls. Jo watched Carole in the light and shadow as she pulled her T shirt up over her head and slipped her skirt off over her hips. And there she was, glorious in her white lace underwear. Legs long and tan. Her new found breasts bursting from their lace prison. Jo was mesmerised by her. Carole was made of curves and fullness and the endless dark mist of her hair. Jo pulled her down onto the blankets with her. Carole lay lazily back, green catlike eyes glowing alluringly under her dark lashes. Jo pulled off her own T shirt and denim shorts. She wore no bra, her own small breasts and hard abdomen stark white against her nut brown suntan- everywhere the sun had been able to reach. She ran her fingers carefully over Carole's body. Goose pimples rose across Carole's skin expanding outwards from where her fingers touched. She reached underneath Carole and released her bra. She pulled down her underwear. Carole looked up at her expectantly. Encouragingly. Knowing what she wanted. She pulled Jo on top of her. Jo's lean body and hipbones pressing into her. Jo's right thigh between Carole's legs pushing at her wetness. Jo's mouth on her mouth. Kissing. Insistent kissing. Unleashing desire on her body. Carole felt Jo's body above hers and the weight of her hunger. Jo moved down her body. Jo's face and sandy head between Carole's thighs, the light flashing stripes across Jo's head. The promise of months becoming real for both of them. Small noises of pleasure that she didn't recognise escaped her lips. Carole felt the world go blurry and a rush of heat to her head and there was a release comparable to nothing she had achieved on her own in her bed. She gripped a handful of Jo's hair and pulled her face into her orgasm.

She let go of Jo's head and smiled. It was amazing. Like no other feeling in the world.

Jo looked up at her, wet glistening around her mouth. She smiled.

They smiled at each other.

It felt like the beginning of something magical.

12

2019

It was a crisp December night for Martin Ashdown's 70th Birthday party. Jo walked to the Ashdown's home and saw the usual bold Christmas lights. She had a royal blue shirt on that she had dug from the back of her wardrobe and some black jeans that if anything she thought were too tight. Although there she was, wearing them. She had straightened her hair in her bedroom mirror and trimmed it a bit around the face with kitchen scissors before she pushed it behind her ears. Jo wasn't someone who visited a hairdressers often. She even had mascara on. She couldn't remember the last time she got this dressed up. This was all for Carole. The woman who had ended things and broken her heart so many years ago. The woman who Jo had been absolutely in love with so many years ago. First love. Best love. It had always been about Carole really. There had been others over the years, but none that felt like Carole. None that felt as right as Carole. None that felt as magical as Carole.

She knocked on the door and waited.

It opened and Anne welcomed her in. Big ash blonde hair and layers of make up. Her perfume overpowering. Another Ashdown party. More champagne. More random people. Again, the only reason Jo was there was for her. And then she saw her, laughing on the sofa. Dazzlingly social as usual. Her dark hair was just above her shoulders in almost casual waves. There were some rich caramel highlights that were new and suited her effortless glamour. Her ruby lipstick had become a part of her. Something she always wore. The carefree teenager was in there some- where. Jo just wanted to find her again. Her Carole. The real Carole, before every- thing else was layered on top.

"JoJo," said Carole warmly. She smiled and pulled Jo close. Hugged her for a second too long. Her lips at Jo's neck and her familiar scent seductive as ever. So many memories attached to her. Jo wanted to bury herself in her hair and float away.

Carole wore a red wool dress. It clung to her body demanding to be looked at. And it was. Some creepy friend of Martin's was all over her. Jo couldn't figure if he didn't realise that Carole was gay or he knew and didn't care. Carole was her usual public self. The self she had spent years developing. The self that flirted and seduced wherever she went. The self that used the way she looked to her advantage. Jo wondered who the real Carole was now. Who are any of us really? Jo was so much more guarded than her teenage self. Which was the real one? When you spent so many years creating a version of yourself for the world to see, did you become that? Jo hoped that Carole hadn't become that. Jo hoped that somewhere underneath the glamorous persona, the Carole that she loved was still there.

They drank champagne and made general conversation. Still in an awkward three way with this older man who couldn't stop staring at Carole's breasts. Not that Jo hadn't noticed them. But Jo was always watching Carole's eyes. She always thought she could tell what Carole was really thinking just from her eyes. Jo hated social occasions. Really hated them.

The older she got, the more she hated them. There was so much pretence and falseness.

They made it through a couple of hours of small talk. So many people Jo sort of knew. So many people interested in the farm. So many people who knew her father and asked about him.

Jo almost ran out of lies to tell.

"Yes, the farm is going well. The ewes are all in lamb. We are looking forward to a good year next year."

"Yes, Dad is well. He is sorry he couldn't make it tonight. He had a long standing arrangement with an old friend this weekend."

"Yes such a shame he couldn't be here."

Jo didn't know where to start. The farm was a mess. She didn't know how she was going to afford another year. Worse than that, she was avoiding doing any-thing about it. Her father had left her with a crumbling mess of a business. They owed a lot of money and Jo had no idea how to even start clearing her debts.

Her father. Arthur. So unwell. Having a conversation with him was a game of patience and repetition. He would cycle through the same questions. What had she been doing that morning? Had she had any lunch? He had forgotten that his wife was dead. And that was so many years ago. If anything that was the one blessing. He had forgotten the biggest tragedy of his life. He had forgotten the pain of losing her. Jo would give almost anything to forget the pain of losing her.

Arthur was a proud man and she knew that he wouldn't want people to know about his illness. She didn't know for how long she could continue to hide the truth, but the least she could do was to hide it for now. To avoid people wanting to visit him and pity him.

Everyone called her Joanna at parties

like this. A name that wasn't really her. A pretence that wasn't really her. It was an acting challenge of pretending to be the Joanna Dale that they thought they knew. The Joanna Dale they wanted to see at the party. The only one who really knew her was Carole.

It was 10.30pm and finally the dinner and the speeches were done.

"JoJo will you just come and have a look at Murphy? I think his paw looked a bit sore earlier." Carole asked.

"Of course." Jo replied and followed Carole out through the kitchen and out to the garage where Murphy was. He was delighted to see them and showed absolutely no sign of a sore paw. Jo sat on his bed with him laughing as the old labrador licked her face in an excited doggy welcome.

"He remembers you." Carole said. "You were always his favourite."

Jo had a good feel of his paws as Carole couldn't remember which paw it allegedly was. Then she looked up at Carole and became aware that there was nothing wrong with Murphy. Carole's bold green eyes said she wanted to get her alone and Murphy was an excuse.

"Jo. I was just thinking. Do you want to get out of here? We've done our bit at this party. I was wondering if maybe we could walk across to yours and catch up properly?"

Jo looked up at her. At her seductive eyes and her ruby lips. Jo never had had and never would have a will or a way to say no to Carole.

"Sure. Although, look at you," Jo said, looking at Carole's high heels, tights, dress. "You can't walk across the fields like that."

Carole laughed. "Well, maybe not exactly like this," she said, kicking off her heels and wandering to a shelf full of assorted boots.

"Ta-da." she said as she slipped her feet into some old Hunter wellington boots covered in a dusting of cobwebs. "You underestimate me." Carole pulled on an old waterproof jacket too.

Jo laughed. "How long since you have worn those?"

"Oh, I don't know. More than ten years probably. Still fit though!"

Jo retrieved her bag and coat and changed her own boots.

"Come on then, don't keep me waiting!" Carole said as she ran out across the driveway and climbed the field gate.

Jo followed. Smiling properly. Feeling suddenly like they had rewound so many years. Feeling like they were the Carole and Jo of teenage years again. Feeling like anything could be possible. They held hands and set off across the fields.

"Is there something wrong with your Dad?" Carole asked as they walked, the night sky clear and open above them.

Jo looked to her, surprised, then re-alised that it was Carole who knew her the best of all. Carole who somehow saw through her.

"He has moved into a care home. He has dementia of some kind. He had been getting a little worse recent years but this year he has just fallen away completely. I was trying so hard to look after him at home, but he is such a liability now. Numerous times I have had to take car keys off him or stop him from getting in a tractor. He has no idea, you see. He thinks he is absolutely fine. Time and time again he would go to cook something and leave it on the stove or in the oven. I rescued a lot of them but we had a small kitchen fire in August- scrambled eggs that he forgot about. I was out working on the harvest, just too far from home and it was only a dog walker seeing smoke and calling 999 that saved his life. And the house from burning down. The firefighters sorted the fire and got him out of there, but seriously Carole. It was so close. If that dog walker hadn't been there.... Anyway, so it was after that really. I wish so much I could care for him but I just can't. I have to be out so much running the farm. So it was then that difficult decisions had to be made. I go and see him every day. But he's just so out of it now. You can't really have a normal conversation with him."

"God, I'm so sorry Jo. This must be horrendous for you. I had no idea."

"Nobody does. I just don't think he would want people to know. I mean, I guess they will find out eventually, but I just don't know how to tell anyone. I just really don't know what to say. I think your father has some idea. He hasn't seen him for a long time and he knows I am running everything now." Jo looked forlorn in the darkness as she spoke. Carole's heart broke as she felt for Jo. Carole squeezed her hand. Poor Jo, whose mother died suddenly when she was so young. Poor Jo, whose father was so ill. And Carole thought of her own family life. Still the warm, comfortable family home. Still both of her parents the same as ever. She had her distance from her family for her own protection. She saw them only very occasionally for she still carried the wounds from her youth. The wounds she feared would never heal. She wondered if she would feel differently towards her parents if she was in the situation that Jo was. That tragedy had struck her home again and again. She didn't know. That was the curious thing about life and illness and death. You never knew who it was going to take next.

Jo opened the door to Westdale Farmhouse and immediately Roux was all over them both, excitement unbound as she jumped and squeaked and rolled on her back. They both pulled their boots off and Carole petted the red and white collie as she looked around her at the demise of Westdale. She hadn't been there in years and the lonely cold house was beginning to fall apart. She saw the smoke damage in the kitchen around the cooker where the fire had been. She saw the dirt and the mess that said that nobody had visited in a long time. She saw the pile of unopened mail, some with bold red stamps angrily proclaiming that the debt was overdue. She took in the sadness and shame on Jo's face. The big dark eyes that looked to her desperately for acceptance.

"I'm so sorry about the mess." Jo said. "Its just me and Roux here now. And she doesn't mind so much." Jo looked down and tried to hide it as a tear escaped down her cheek.

Carole saw Jo's 16 year old self in front of her suddenly. Skinny girl frame with big sad dead mum eyes. Jo was still in so much pain. More pain. So many years later. So much time had passed. And now she was all alone in the big house.

And just like years ago, Carole wanted only to care for her. Only to love her. Only to make it all okay somehow. Something about the fragility underneath Jo's quiet strength had always awoken this side of Carole. This side that never made the light of day. This side of the powerful business woman that nobody knew.

Carole pulled Jo to her and kissed her. It was the first time she had kissed anyone in years. For Carole, kissing was the most intimate act. She held Jo's face in her hands and tenderly kissed her lips. Kissed the tears from her cheek. Kissed her pain away. She sat down on the bottom of the staircase and Jo collapsed into her arms sobbing. Jo cried the pain of years, her face against Carole's breast, her tears soaking into Carole's wool dress. Carole saw the grey hairs that were appearing on Jo's head.

Carole held her as the minutes passed, Jo buried her face into Carole and it felt like home. For both of them. Carole could smell Jo's hair, it always smelt of strawberries. It brought back old memories. When Jo's tears subsided a bit, she looked up to Carole and they kissed. Years of desire and pain and loss swept away in the kiss. Jo stood and offered her hand to Carole leading her upstairs. She still slept in the same bedroom as she did as a child. A farmhouse with so many rooms and nothing about Jo's room had changed. Not really. Still the photos of Jo's dogs everywhere. Still the same old wooden framed bed they had shared often that beautiful summer many years ago. As "friends" officially. Friends who touched each other under the quiet blanket of darkness.

The wallpaper aged and peeling now. The carpet worn away to nothing in places. Her bedroom didn't seem dirty at least. Ironically, even though Carole's beautiful London flat was always immaculate, she realised in that moment that it was Jo's bedroom that felt like home. Perhaps the only place she had ever felt really at home. In Jo's arms was home.

The two women collapsed into the bed together. Their bodies changed over the years but still so familiar. Clothes peeled off and they made their way under the duvet- the house was cold.

They kissed tenderly. Then hungrily. Feeling the other's nakedness against their own. Their bodies speaking for them, asking for what they had wanted for so many years. Carole felt almost self conscious for the first time in years. Aware that her body had thickened over the years. Aware that she was different than the last time she was naked with Jo. Then suddenly she realised that it didn't matter. That Jo wanted her regardless. That Jo was still, as Jo always had been, dizzy with lust for her. Carole rolled on top of Jo kissing her. Her hand reached down over Jo's pubic thatch, feeling her passion. Carole's slim manicured fingers moved skilfully into Jo's wetness, teasing, playing, well practiced over the years. She tried to remember what Jo liked so many years ago, she wished she knew more about her, sure to have changed and developed in her tastes over the years. She pushed her fingers into Jo. Jo's pupils widened in the shadows, deep with want and need. Carole responded and went into a smooth rhythm into her and out, her lips just above Jo's as Jo gasped in pleasure. Jo's back arched and her small nipples stood proud, her legs thrown apart as she gave in to the depth of feeling and orgasm crashed over her body as sure as the ocean crashes to the shore. She dissolved into nothing and curled up fetal. And Carole held her close. Holding Jo's vulnerability. Kissing her hair. Whispering in her ear.

"Everything will be ok. I've got you."

But did she have her? Did she really have her this time? Jo felt herself falling. But did she trust Carole to catch her this time?

13

1995

It was August, nearing the end of the school summer holidays and Jo and Carole were inseparable. Jo had work to do on the farm helping with the harvest and the sheep and Carole would help. Jo's father always happy to have another pair of hands and he always liked Carole. She might not look the part, but she always worked hard and that was what was important to Arthur. Carole somehow still looked glamorous after a day on the farm, glossy hair shining in a ponytail, her feminine face somehow not as sweaty and dirty as anyone else's. In the evenings she would soak her hands and moisturise them and was forever re-painting her nails. She was the only one to somehow escape 'workers hands'. Jo often marvelled as she held Carole's hands in her own how perfect her hands were. How delicate her long fingers were. How beautiful her short and neatly painted and filed nails were. On the evenings they would stay in each other's beds. Their parents extremely naive to what was going on. Carole's parents liked Carole's 'best friend'. Jo was a polite, quiet girl and Anne in particular had so much sympathy for Jo's situation.

"Terrible thing for a child to go through, losing her mother." Anne would often say. "So lovely of you to help Joanna, Carole. She will be in such dreadful pain now, it is good that you are such a good friend to her."

And so they would spend evenings in

Carole's bedroom. It would always get the evening sun and they would lounge on her bed talking and laughing. They played board games and listened to music and moved their hands swiftly away from each other when Anne poked her head round the door. Anne was so proud of Carole. She was developing perfectly. She was beautiful and never difficult, she did well at school and she was not getting into trouble with boys, although a lot of men were becoming very interested in her. Anne had no doubt that Carole would grow up and find a very eligible husband.

It was funny, Carole thought that she never really had had any close friends before Jo. Jo was everything to her, the one person she felt really herself around. She spent so much time playing a role of the 'young lady' that was so important to both of her parents, she felt like she had spent years masking who she really was. The image she projected was what was so important to her parents, not who she really was.

They would ostensibly put pyjamas on and brush their teeth and each others hair and say goodnight to Carole's parents like good girls. As if they were twelve years old. And Carole's parents would believe them as they got an early night like good girls. The lights went out and they slipped under the duvet. Anne Ashdown would be downstairs cleaning or baking late at night usually. Very distracted. Martin Ashdown would watch TV late into the evening, a whisky in his hand, the ice cubes clunked together as he sipped it.

Upstairs under cover of pyjamas and duvets and darkness, the good girls would play. Carole's fingers slipping into Jo's shorts. Jo's mouth to Carole's nipple. Carole's hand in Jo's hair. They fucked quietly in Carole's house. Secretly. Jo's hand over Carole's mouth as she came and gushed wetness onto a towel. Jo's face in the pillow as Caroles mouth brought her to orgasm. Quiet pleasure. Tiny gasps and groans. And in the morning towels smelling of sex would be buried deep in the washing basket for Anne to wash. They would shower again and smell fresh as they came down for breakfast. Anne would plate up hot bacon and egg sandwiches to feed the good girls up for their day on the farm and Jo and Carole would smile conspiratorially across the kitchen table.

Good girls. Bad girls. Good girls.

1995

A hard day on the farm and the girls would catch moments where they could. The excitement of their secret affair never dulled. Stolen kisses on a tractor. A quick brush of hands. Loaded glances.

Harvest was a busy time and there was

no end of work but there were always moments when they were alone together. Alone in the hay barn where they first had sex. It was both of their virginities lost. They would smile at the thought. They would laugh as they fell into the bed of hay together. Their kisses eager, their hunger too much, clothes would be off and their hands and mouths would bring each other to orgasm so quickly. Their sex felt like the most natural, easiest thing in the world. It was only as they grew up and had different sexual partners that they would realise that it just wasn't always like that. That sometimes, you just aren't compatible in what you want with someone. That sometimes, orgasm isn't that easy to achieve- either in yourself or in others. But, with the beautiful optimism of youth, neither of them saw that. Neither of them imagined being with anyone else. The magic between them seemed just too strong. Just too unbreakable.

Arthur started taking sleeping pills following his wife's death. When he went to bed, the girls could be completely sure he was totally out of it until 6am when he would rise like clockwork.

They took advantage of this when they slept over in Jo's bed.

It was the last day of summer before Carole had to go away again back to college. The girls had worked hard on the farm in the day. They made it back to Westdale Farm knowing Arthur would be out for another couple of hours.

Jo ran a bath. The big cast iron farmhouse bath was soon deep with hot water and fruity smelling bubbles. The two of them stripped their dirty clothes. Jo watched Carole undress every chance she got. Literally entranced by her curves. She adored Carole's body. Carole stepped into the bath gracefully. Her long legs slim and tanned. Her breasts floated in the bubbles. She watched Jo too, although she would never tell her or Jo would get self conscious. Jo's skinny frame was filling out, gaining muscle particularly through the shoulders and arms and Carole watched her strong arms work as she lowered herself into the other end of the bath.

Jo slipped under the water to fully submerge herself and wet her hair and her face. Carole touched between her legs as she was under the water and she spluttered and came up laughing.

"You look good wet, JoJo." Carole said seductively.

"Wet from the water?" Jo asked.

"Wet any which way." Carole answered nonchalantly.

Jo went bright red and awkward. Carole had always had this talent to be so disarming. So quick and clever with her words. Knowing exactly how to reduce Jo to a puddle of lust at any time.

Carole splashed bubbles at her.

Jo smiled. She was so happy with Carole. She would miss her so much when she had to go back to school. But there was always the next holidays. Then Christmas holidays. They had plans for how it would work. They had plans for Carole coming home.

"Massage my feet please JoJo." Carole asked. Jo took her neatly pedicured foot and massaged it. Always so keen to please Carole. Always so keen to do anything Carole wanted. Seeing Carole's happiness gave Jo so much pleasure.

Carole stretched her long leg out and Jo moved her hands up Carole's leg. Rubbing her leg. Moving higher. Her fingers exploring under the water. Carole's breathing quickening and her satisfaction evident. Carole's body responded so well to her touch. Carole moaned for her. Jo was soon fucking her and Carole knew they had the house to themselves and wasn't bound by silence. Carole's orgasm was loud and long. The sound of Carole's orgasm and the way her body shook and her head rolled back was like heroin itself to Jo. Or like she imagined heroin might feel like. The highest of highs.

She leant in and kissed Carole deeply and they both relaxed into the bubbles.

Then the girls washed each others hair, gently. Tenderly. They shaved each others bodies. Legs, armpits, between each others legs. There was absolute intimacy and beauty in doing it for each other. The razor running smoothly over tanned skin. The razor running intricately over sensitive folds between their legs. Their trust in each other implicit and unspoken.

The bath water was cool by the time they got out. Hot bodies into bed next to each other. Pyjamas not necessary in Westdale Farmhouse. Arthur would never come to Jo's room.

More sex in bed together. Their last night together. Sweet sex. Passionate sex.

Rough sex. And everything in between. They would orgasm, then rest in each others arms, then go again. Jo and Carole couldn't get enough of each other. They finally fell asleep, satiated and exhausted. Tanned bodies intertwined. Smiling into each others hair.

"I love you JoJo." mumbled Carole.

"I love you too." replied Jo.

They felt like the most natural three words in the world.

Their love felt like it should have been enough.

14

2019

The morning after Martin Ashdown's 70th birthday party and Jo's stolen overnight with Carole, Carole had to leave and drive back to London. The trouble with a job like Carole's was that it never really stopped. The responsibility of being in charge never really lapsed.

The new office that had opened in Sydney needed Carole's help. Carole was back to London and back to work. She could run the world from anywhere really. All she needed was her laptop and some good Wifi, but being at home with her parents there just wasn't the peace. And Jo. There was Jo. Carole had been thinking more and more about Jo over recent years. Finally spending the night with her again after all that time, all the love, all the sadness. Hearing about her father and seeing the obvious state that Westdale Farm was in. What now? She had re-opened an old box of memories on a whim and she hadn't planned beyond that first night. She had had no idea Jo still felt the same way that she did. She had had no idea how strongly she herself felt and it terrified her. She had had no idea how much of a mess Jo was in. She didn't expect Jo to respond so emotionally to her. She didn't realise how much depth of feeling was still there.

It seemed so much easier just to go back to London, to her lovely apartment and to bury herself in work rather than to think of Jo and the future and what it could possibly mean. It wasn't realistic anyway. Carole couldn't operate from the countryside, she was a city girl these days. She had lived in the city now longer than she had on the farm.

JO SAT ALONE in the old farmhouse kitchen with a cup of tea contemplating her life choices. She had been so foolish to take Carole back to her bed after so many years. She had cried on Carole, she had fucked Carole, Carole had seen way too much about the mess she was living in. Jo vowed never to drink champagne again. It all seemed like a good idea at the time. Being around Carole was fatal to Jo. Carole dazzled brighter than the sun itself and yet nothing good had ever come of loving Carole. Heartbreak was what came from loving Carole. Jo was stupid to make herself vulnerable to Carole again and expect a different result. She hadn't heard

from her since she left. Things were awkward the morning after. The magic from
the night before had faded and they were
both left shell shocked by what had
happened.

CAROLE HAD TOLD her as she left that she
needed to open her mail. The pile of letters Jo had been avoiding had got pretty
high. She took a deep breath and opened
the first one. From the farm machinery
mechanics.

YOUR ACCOUNT IS OVERDUE. YOU
OWE £3243. PAY BY 3RD DECEMBER OR
YOUR ACCOUNT WILL BE PASSED TO
DEBT COLLECTORS.

THE NEXT LETTER was from the bank
saying she had exceeded her overdraft
and would be charged every day.

The next letter from the feed merchants where she bought the feed for the pregnant ewes over the winter asking her to settle her account immediately or they would no longer serve her.

More letters, more demands for money.

Jo put her head in her hands. There was no way out. She would need to sell something to pay the debts. But what this time? Some more land? There wasn't that much left and without the land she wouldn't be able to raise the sheep and grow the crops.

Or there was Roux. Roux's loyal red head was on her lap.

She had been offered £15,000 for Roux but had turned it down immediately. Many other farmers had wanted Roux. She was the best sheepdog in the country. She was probably worth even more than that with so much potential to work and to breed pups from an exceptional bloodline, but even the thought of losing her broke Jo. She cried and broke down on the floor, sobbing into Roux's furry mane. Roux licked her tears. It reminded her of Carole kissing her tears last night. Her soft lips against Jo's face. Her tenderness. Her love. It just made her cry more thinking of losing her all over again.

Martin Ashdown had regularly told her just to come to him if she needed money, that they could work something out. And she had been to him. And each time he had helped her out. But each time he had taken something valuable from her. Taking apart Westdale Farm piece by piece. Jo wondered how many years it would be until he took it all from her. Her farm. Her livelihood. Her home. And then what? What next when it was all gone?

CAROLE, back in her apartment, turned on

the shower. Carole liked the shower as hot as it would go. Burning down and cleansing her. She stripped her clothes off and inhaled. She could still smell Jo on her skin. She could still smell sex on her fingers.

Enough.

She reluctantly stepped in the shower to wash Jo away. Cleansing her body and hoping to cleanse her mind. There was no future for her with Jo.

15

1995

Carole was home for Christmas. They had spoken most days while Carole had been away. Carole on a payphone calling Jo on the landline at the farm. There had been no privacy but hearing each other's voices had been everything. There had also been letters of a much more explicit nature. Jo had her letters from Carole hidden away in a box under her bed. Not that her father would have noticed. He was a broken man after losing his wife. His grief gradually eroding him. Jo had distracted herself from the loss of her mother with Carole. She was completely immersed in Carole.

Carole had been home for a few days before Christmas and they had gone right back to how things were before she left. Obsessed with each other. Spending every hour they could together awake or asleep. Sex, everywhere they could and as much as they could. They couldn't get enough of each other.

On Christmas day, there was snow. Only a little, but it's soft white covering made the countryside into a magical world. Jo and Arthur were invited again to Manor Farm for Christmas day.

Jo had slept at Westdale Farm on Christmas Eve with her father. It seemed the right thing to do. Jo and Arthur walked across the snowy fields on Christmas morning. Jo wished the dogs could have come, but Anne didn't like dogs in the house.

. . .

THE ASHDOWNS' extended family and friends came and went. But Jo didn't mind this year. She had Carole so everything was OK. Carole was radiant in a gold blouse and a tight black skirt. Jo couldn't take her eyes off her. They escaped for a pre Christmas lunch walk together under guise of taking the dogs out and Carole lead Jo back to where they had walked the year before. Back to sit on the same fallen tree next to the river. The same light snow around them. Everything changed between them. They held each others hands and kissed.

"I got you a present." Jo said. She fished into her pocket and pulled out a small box messily wrapped.

Carole smiled, her red lips ever seductive and pulled a smaller box from her own pocket. Only hers was obviously immaculately wrapped.

They exchanged gifts and unwrapped them.

Jo opened hers to find a top of the range shepherd's whistle on a neck chain engraved with tiny letters:

JoJo
love C

16

1995

"Thank you so much this is perfect!" Jo's face lit up with delight. It shone solid silver in the light. It would last her her whole life. She put it to her lips and blew. The dogs pricked their ears up. Jo put it round her neck straight away, she had never had a present that she loved more.

Carole opened hers and another silver chain shone. A delicate silver chain with a snowflake charm on it.

"It reminded me of you. Of us." Jo said. "Of last Christmas when we came out here and you held my hands and kissed them. You gave me this hope. That everything might be okay. And I thought maybe you would like it. "

Carole smiled. "Well, you had better put it on me then." Carole turned her back to Jo and lifted her hair up. The nape of her neck was as graceful as a swan. Jo fumbled with her cold hands and fastened the necklace around Carole's neck. She turned back around.

"How do I look?" Carole asked. The snowflake glinted on her chest. Her blouse's neckline showing the cleavage of her breasts.

"You look incredible." Jo said pulling her close and kissing her.

They were lost again in one another, kissing, laughing, warming cold hands under each others clothes.

∼

LATER THAT EVENING, Christmas night, Arthur went home and Jo stayed with Carole. They put Christmas pyjamas on. They drank Baileys while the grown ups napped on the sofa. They went upstairs to Carole's warm bed and quickly Carole was on top of Jo. Kissing Jo. Pulling Jo's pyjama shorts down and working her way down between her legs.

"Merry Christmas JoJo."

"Merry Christmas Carole."

They lay in each others arms afterwards. Lost in an orgasmic haze. They were so happy. They were so close. They felt like nothing could ever take that away from them.

They had no idea what was coming.

17

2019

Carole was working from home the week before Christmas. She put her thick coat on and sat out on her balcony with her laptop enjoying the cold river air and the view.

A new email flashed up from the company director. She clicked it open.

Carole,
We are delighted with the work you did in
Sydney earlier in the year. We would like to
offer you the position of Managing Director of

Redwall in Australia. You would be in charge
of all operations in Australia and of growing
the Australian arm of Redwall.
I am happy to discuss with you a resettlement
package, an incredible apartment in Sydney
and a very generous salary and I am sure
that we can agree on something you will find
very acceptable.
Please take time to consider this offer
carefully. It will absolutely be the explosion of
your career and the beginning of everything
you have worked for.

Carole was stunned. This really was an
offer beyond what she had thought was
possible. She loved her time in Sydney
and it really was the career move she
wanted to make. It was the new start she
had thought about for years.

IT WOULD TAKE her away from all these
ridiculous feelings for Jo. She could escape and not deal with any of it.

Since getting back to London she had spoken to Jo only briefly. Everything was awkward. There had been a couple of texts but she didn't know what she wanted so she was avoiding it. Avoiding Jo. Avoiding decisions. And yet, here was another decision.

Move to Sydney in the career move of the century or not?

18

1995

It was Boxing day, the day after Christmas, and Jo had gone home to see her father. Carole had wanted to go too but Anne said she needed her at home to help with some chores around the house. Jo set off home across the fields, the weight of her world felt so much lighter with Carole to bear it with her.

Anne and Martin sat at the kitchen table.

"Carole. Sit down. We need to talk to

you. It is important," said Martin, his shirt loose around his neck, his voice strained.

Carole sat down curious and scared of what was to come. Wondering what on earth it could be, but both of her parents were deathly serious.

Anne threw onto the table a handful of letters.

Letters from Jo.

The letters that were hidden in Carole's suitcase that Jo had sent her while she had been away.

Love letters.

Sexually explicit letters.

Carole's world began to crumble around her.

"We heard you last night. You and Joanna." Anne said sternly, her face going redder and redder.

"We know what you have done. What you have both done." Martin stammered.

"Lesbian." Anne choked out.

That didn't even make sense. Not a sentence. Not a question. Accusatory.

"I love her." Carole said quietly.

"I DON'T CARE." Martin shouted. He had always been a man quick to anger. Almost like two separate people. He was aggressive. He stood up. "It is over. This thing with the Dale girl. This lesbian thing. You won't see her or speak to her. You absolutely will not be a lesbian. Your mother and I will not accept it."

ANNE STARTED TO CRY. "Disgusting. So disgusting and unnatural. I can't believe you would do something like that Carole. You've broken my heart."

Carole didn't know what to do. She started trying to defend herself. To defend Jo. But it was futile. The two of them came back at her angrier and angrier. More and more upset.

"No daughter of mine will bring

shame on our family. You need to think about your priorities young lady. This stops. Right now. There will be absolutely no contact."

"No Dad. Please. I love her." Carole cried.

"CAROLE, this nonsense stops. Right now. You will go back to school. I'll find work for you somewhere far away for the easter holidays and the summer holidays. Then you go to university and make something of your life. You can come home for Christmas, but that is it. Do not dare to disobey me. You do not want to know what will happen."

"No Dad...." she cried.

"Do as your father says," Anne screamed.

There was an empty moment when nobody spoke.

"I've packed your bags. Your father is

driving you to London where you will stay with your uncle until term starts. You won't come anywhere near Joanna Dale. There will be no more of this."

Carole sobbed into her hands at the futility of the situation. She wanted nothing more than to run away and be with Jo. But this wasn't a world where women had relationships with women. She didn't know a single lesbian. No celebrities. Nobody she knew.

Her father threw her suitcase into the Range Rover and told her to get in the car.

Carole didn't move.

"Get in the car. I won't ask again."

CAROLE DIDN'T MOVE. He slapped her hard in the face. His right hand connecting with her cheekbone and her head and whole body knocked sideways with the force. Anne looked away. Pain rung through Caroles skull. He grabbed a handful of her long hair and dragged her into the vehicle as she screamed and cried. He threw her in the back seat as though she was another bag. He hit her again and his fist connected with her ribs. And again. And again. She cowered into a ball and cried as he slammed the door. She lay quietly crying the whole journey to London. Neither of them spoke at all. No more words were needed. His violence towards her said everything.

Carole was in shock in her new surroundings for days. Her cheek and eye socket was purple and blue and bruising also dappled her ribcage. She had no idea what to do. She wasn't allowed anywhere near the phone to call Jo. Her uncle watched her like a hawk. She eventually managed to steal a piece of paper, an envelope, a stamp and a pen from his desk and wrote a letter to Jo. She couldn't find the words to say. The letter was cold and empty. Carole had no more tears left to cry. She had no more feelings left to feel. She couldn't think of Jo now. She just had to think about surviving her new life without Jo.

Dear JoJo,

I know there is no way to rectify the harm that I have caused you by disappearing. There are no words to tell you how I feel right now or to apologise enough for what I need to say to you.

It is over between us. My parents found your letters to me. I cannot be with you anymore. There is no us anymore. I'm going away for a long time.

I wish you nothing but the best in everything in life. You deserve all good things. Please move on with your life.

I'll always care for you, but there can never be anything further between us.

With love,
Carole

CAROLE MANAGED to get let out for a walk and slip the letter into a postbox. A woman with a small child saw her bruised face and gasped. Then she looked away awkwardly. The man in the shop looked at her then looked away too. Carole soon found that people look at you differently when you are a woman with facial bruising. People looked at her differently and she was different. A different self.

No longer a carefree child. She had had a welcome to the real world and she hated everything about it. She would have to find a new way to survive. But she daren't disobey her father. She feared how far he would go.

Jo HAD BEEN frantic wondering why Carole didn't meet her when she was supposed to. On calling Carole's home, Anne answered and said coldly, "Carole has gone away. She will be gone for a long time. Please don't call again." Then Anne hung up.

Jo was torn in confusion and pain.

Where was Carole? What on earth had happened?

She never doubted Carole or that Carole would come back to her until she received the letter days later.

Carole was gone.

Carole was really gone.

Their relationship was over and she had no way to contact her or find out what had happened. She had no idea where Carole was.

Jo couldn't believe that Carole wouldn't fight for them despite her parents finding out. But, she hadn't. Whatever happened, Carole had given up on them.

Carole had broken her heart.

19

2019

There had been no snow that winter. Global warming had a lot to answer for. Christmas Day was sunny in fact. But still cold. Jo had no idea where things were at between her and Carole. Jo visited her father first thing. He had his Christmas jumper on. He looked happy and seemed to know it was Christmas Day, although he kept asking where Jo's mother was, still so sure she was alive. Again, Jo played along and didn't have the heart to tell him anything otherwise. Jo and Roux went out for a late morning walk. The air cold against her face. Jo's business was still in a mess. She had made no decisions. Going to Martin felt like going to the lion's den and offering parts of her own body as snacks for him. How long until she had nothing left to give? And then what?

Roux ran across the field, a streak of red and white. Jo wished she had a dog's life. That simple joy of running though the fields, just happy to be alive and outside. Maybe there was a time in her life when she had felt like that too. But not now. Not anymore. She felt so alone.

CAROLE HAD ARRIVED back at her parents house late on Christmas eve. She hugged both her parents and there were pleasantries. Polite conversation as usual. Carole played the role they expected from her. She gave nothing more and nothing less. As she had done for many years. Played the dutiful daughter.

"I'm tired. I'm going to get an early night." Carole said. She took her overnight bag upstairs with her and headed to her childhood bedroom. The decor had changed as Anne redecorated, but her bed was the same as always. The wardrobe and drawers were full of her things from years ago. Hidden away, but right there below the surface if you scratched hard enough.

Carole sat on her bed and thought carefully about her life. About her future. She couldn't fake it anymore with her family. She had never forgiven or forgotten what happened that Christmas when she was eighteen. She came home every Christmas since because it was the one day of the year she got to see Jo. She couldn't have Jo, but that way she could check on her every year. See she was okay. But it was no way to live.

Moving to Australia and taking the Sydney job would be the new start she needed. Leaving her shitty family and their expectations behind and finally taking control of her own destiny.

She would tell Jo tomorrow. Explain to her. Tell her everything. Hope she could understand.

She opened her laptop and logged in.

Waited for her email to load then she opened up a new email. Ready to email and accept the Sydney offer.

Her fingers stalled on the keyboard.

She hesitated.

She would send it tomorrow after she had told everyone.

CHRISTMAS DAY

Carole dressed in a slinky emerald green dress that matched her eyes. As she did her makeup, she looked in the mirror at the fine lines that had started to mar her face. She wasn't immune to the aging process.

12 o'clock came and people started arriving. Family. Friends. Carole was effervescent. She was a gifted actress, she had trained for years to play this very part. Only someone who knew her very well would be able to tell that she was dead behind the eyes.

Jo.

Jo would be able to tell that she was dead behind the eyes.

Jo arrived alone and made excuses for Arthur that he wasn't feeling too well. Nobody questioned her and she was relieved at that.

She saw Carole, resplendent in that green dress, but she avoided her. She didn't know what to say. She didn't know what on earth was going on, after what happened last time.

Carole saw Jo arrive and avoid her

gaze. She wished things could be different. They spent the day doing this awkward dance of avoidance. There were enough people there that it wasn't obvious to anyone but themselves.

Carole steeled herself to try and find a way to talk to Jo alone. To try and apologise to her and to explain about the move to Australia.

But she couldn't find the time and she couldn't find the words.

Soon after lunch finished Jo thanked Anne and Martin robotically and said goodbye and set off home. Carole felt her stomach lurch. Her body shook. She needed to speak to Jo. She had to see Jo to explain. She still hadn't told the family about Australia, she had wanted to tell Jo first. She went upstairs determined to send the email and make it real but her fingers stuck on the keyboard. She couldn't type the email.

She felt sick at her very core and she

knew in that second that it was all about Jo.

She couldn't leave her. She couldn't be without her. She couldn't breathe any more without her. There had been too many years and too much emptiness and loss. She went to her window and watched Jo's hunched frame across the field. She had got skinnier in the past couple of weeks, her face had been gaunt and her eye sockets hollow. Jo needed her too. She couldn't be without Jo anymore. She picked up her make up bag, at the bottom of it was just what she was looking for. The snowflake charm glinted and sparkled at her. She had kept it all those years. She put the necklace on.

She ran downstairs, snuck out the back door and pulled her boots on and ran across the field after Jo. Joanna Dale. The love of her life.

"Jo," she called as she ran across the

field. She wasn't fit these days so she was out of breath quickly.

"Jo," she shouted again as she got closer.

Jo turned towards her voice.

"I love you!" Carole shouted.

"What?!" Jo replied in shock.

"I love you JoJo!"

Carole ran the last bit towards a stunned Jo and fell into her arms.

"I'm so sorry for everything. I can explain everything. But I can't be without you. Not again. I am miserable without you. I feel sick at the thought of losing you again. Please Jo. Please. I love you with everything I have and everything I am and I want to spend the rest of my life making it up to you. Please give me another chance."

There was a moment. Just a moment, in the fields, the winter sun high above. Jo looked at Carole. Carole Ashdown, the woman of her every dream and fantasy.

The woman she had thought about every single day since she was sixteen years old. The one who no-one else had ever lived up to. In the beautiful emerald silk dress. With the old muddy welly boots on. With her snowflake chain glinting at her chest. Jo's response didn't take much consideration.

"I love you too. I always have. I literally always have. Every day of my adult life I have loved you, Carole."

Carole held Jo's face and kissed her deeply. The years of pain ebbed away as they kissed.

"I promise you, things will be different now," Carole said.

Jo wanted with every fibre of her being to believe her.

20

2019

They woke up together the next morning. Carole woke to Jo's hands on her body. Her warmth at her back. Jo pushed her hair aside and kissed the back of her neck lightly. Carole tingled all over. Her body suddenly so alive and responsive. Jo's kisses became firmer. Across her shoulder. She pushed Carole onto her front, her face in the pillow and she lay face down on top of her. Her lips at Carole's ear, kissing her ear, sucking her earlobe.

"I want you," she whispered, loud in Carole's ear.

Jo bit her shoulder and Carole winced underneath her. Jo carried on kissing her and licking her, her neck, her shoulder, her back.

Carole had never been more turned on. Jo's weight pressed into her, she felt pinned and taken. She felt vulnerable for the first time in so long. She gave up control willingly to Jo. The one she trusted. Jo ran her hand down over Carole's ass and reached between her legs. Carole was so hot and soaking wet. Carole's own hand reached underneath her body to touch herself too.

Jo positioned herself with pressure on the back of Carole's thigh and they rocked together as Jo's fingers fucked her.

Carole's loud moans were muffled slightly by the pillow. But Jo felt her body tensing underneath her. She knew Carole's body as well as she knew her own. As the wave of orgasm rushed over Carole, it hit Jo too. Her clit tight against the back of Carole's thigh. They came together hard and Jo collapsed on top of her, her lips at her ear.

"You are incredible. I love you, I always have," whispered Jo.

Carole smiled. "I love you too JoJo," she murmured into the pillow, Jo's body holding her close, Jo's strong arms around her.

JO WENT DOWNSTAIRS and came back with coffee for them both, then she folded herself into Carole's arm. Her face against Carole's breast. Her fingers dragged slowly across Carole's skin and circled the snowflake charm. They lay together at peace watching the sun rise through the window.

"I can't believe it has been so long. It

feels like we have always been together." said Jo.

"On some level, we have. I know in my mind we have been. And probably in yours too."

They lay quietly as they thought about it.

"I've been thinking about the farm." said Carole, suddenly business again. "I'm leaving my job. I've had enough. I'm selling my apartment so I will have money to get us going and renovate this house. I was thinking I could run the farm for you. I have some ideas."

"Oh yeah?" said Jo. "What do you know about running farms?"

"JoJo, I could run the world if I wanted to. I'm a business and marketing expert. A farm isn't so different from any other business you know? We would do it together of course. But I was thinking of a change of plans. How would you feel about putting a dog boarding kennels into the big barn? A dog hotel. We could make it nice, luxury. We could put deer fencing in around a couple of fields and put them to grass so the dogs had somewhere secure to exercise and play. We will make a much more reliable income by boarding dogs. I was thinking you could also take in sheep-dogs for training. You are a gifted dog trainer, you know that don't you? And a well trained sheepdog is worth its weight in gold to the right people."

"How will we find the customers?" asked Jo, excited but still not sure.

Carole smiled that smile of hers that said she knew exactly what she was doing and everything would be ok.

"Jo, thats my thing. I get the cus-tomers. I'll get you more customers than you know what to do with. All you will have to do is train the dogs!"

And suddenly it seemed like there was a light at the end of the tunnel. Carole was a force of nature, if she said these things would happen then she would make them happen.

The weight of the world lifted from Jo's shoulders.

"Firstly, I'm going to tell my parents about us. Then, we are going to start cleaning up around here. I can't live like this! You can get started on the kitchen while I am out. We are going to bin everything that we don't need or want and then clean and scrub everything. Okay?" Carole said.

Jo smiled and it all seemed somehow achievable with Carole there to organise and plan and make stuff happen.

"Also, I was thinking, once we have cleaned up a bit, we could get your Dad to move back home, if you wanted. I can do most of my work from home. You won't have to work such long hours. We can look after him together if you want. I'll make sure he gets into no trouble." Carole was the woman with all the answers once again.

Jo smiled genuinely and widely. "He would love to come home. I would love to have him home."

"Then we will make it happen. Anything is possible you know."

Jo didn't know. Not before. But, with Carole by her side, anything seemed suddenly possible.

CAROLE STOOD in Manor Farm kitchen, her childhood home and prepared to tell her parents about her relationship with Jo and she was prepared for literally any response. It had taken her twenty four years to stand up to them finally after her scars from the last time. Twenty four years of pain. So much was unspoken and remained unspoken. Her fear of her father had taken its toll. Even though she was now very much an adult and a powerful woman, it had taken her so long to make this step. It was the hardest thing she had done of her own choosing. He had had so much control over her for so long. She flinched as she told them, almost expecting to incite a violent rage in him similar to the one so many years ago.

"I'm in love with Jo and I am going to be living with her starting from now. I'm moving up from London to be with her."

They all stood in the same farmhouse kitchen as her parents took in the information.

They didn't really react this time. It was the strangest thing. It was the biggest anticlimax. Martin said nothing.

Anne paused a moment. Looked to Martin.

Then said, "That's nice dear. Maybe we will see you more often. Did you get much chance to speak to Simon and Alice yesterday darling? They were very much looking forward to seeing you."

The subject was changed and the moment was done.

In the years that had passed they had obviously found their own way to cope with their daughter being a lesbian.

Carole couldn't believe the years she had spent worrying about that day. About ever coming out to them again. About the consequences of being with Jo ever again. She made her excuses and left quickly, not looking back. Heading back across the fields to her new home. She was angry. Angry that they had taken the best years of her life with that one day. That one day after Christmas so long ago. They had no idea how badly they had hurt her.

She wished for a second for another family. That she had different parents. Then she thought of Jo and what had happened to her family. A different pain.

Maybe, it was just a lottery. Maybe we all come out damaged one way or another.

Now her damaged soul had Jo's damaged soul and things were different. She had made her own family. As she got back towards the house Jo and Roux rushed out to greet her. Jo's smile was wide and she hugged Carole and held her tight.

"Merry Christmas JoJo."

"Merry Christmas you," Jo laughed.

They stood together in the driveway and they felt like teenagers again. They were overwhelmed with happiness and anything felt possible. They had their whole lives ahead of them.

THE END

ABOUT THE AUTHOR

Margaux Fox

Hey everyone, I just want to thank you so much for reading my book. I would love for you to pop on Amazon and review it if you enjoyed it. As an indie author, reviews really do make a difference and get my books noticed and would be hugely appreciated.

I grew up on a farm and have always adored Border Collies, so I always wanted to write a story based on a farm. I pestered my dad for years and eventually got my own collie called Jake who I absolutely adored. We did everything together.

Mailing List!

Please sign up to my mailing list to be the first to know about new releases and to learn about the background of the stories I create:

https://aw16b97e.aweberpages.com/p/ 7b489e6f-aaa0-4c10-949b-b4b1f4e4aa74

Go and give me a follow on Social Media and don't be afraid to give me any feedback on anything you particularly enjoyed or didn't enjoy about the book.

www.facebook.com/lovefrommargaux

www.instagram.com/lovefrommargaux

www.twitter.com/lovefrommargaux

Or contact me on email:
lovefrommargaux@googlemail.com

Please also check out my other books. All my books are available to read for free on Kindle Unlimited.

Her Royal Bodyguard

What happens when a female bodyguard falls for the Princess she is supposed to be protecting?

Following an accident, Sergeant Erin Kennedy is offered the biggest promotion there is, to become bodyguard to Princess Alexandra, the heir to the British Throne.

Rule Number One of the Bodyguard Handbook: Never fall in love with the client

Princess Alexandra is due to marry a Prince. So, when Erin begins to fall in love with the charismatic Princess, she knows it is only a matter of time before it will end in tears.

Erin finds herself drawn in to the Princess's tangled web of duty, responsibility and secrets.

With the pressure on both women building, how long before they start to break?

Buy in the US: My Book

Buy in the UK: My Book

Buy in Australia: My Book

Buy in Canada: My Book

Falling For Her

Dedicated police detective Jen Towers thought her marriage and her job were everything she wanted. Although thirty years old, and disillusioned with the things she thought she believed in, she would never have imagined she would be lured into a hot affair with the dangerously attractive stranger Lyra.

Her secret relationship with Lyra drags Jen into a web of lies and betrayal.

When it ends in murder, Jen realises she is playing a dangerous game.

Who is left to trust when Jen doesn't even recognise herself anymore?

Buy in the US: My Book

Buy in the UK: My Book

Buy in Australia: My Book

Buy in Canada: My Book

Printed in Great Britain
by Amazon

31325219R10081